For Amanda

When Father Christmas seems too fat
For the chimney,
And you have no more teeth
For the tooth fairy;
There is still some magic in the world
That you can believe in.

AMANDA'S *Butterfly*

NICK BUTTERWORTH

COLLINS

One sunny morning
I woke up before
anyone else in the house.
I sat up in bed and
read a story to my friends.
It was about a butterfly.
The story gave me
a brilliant idea...

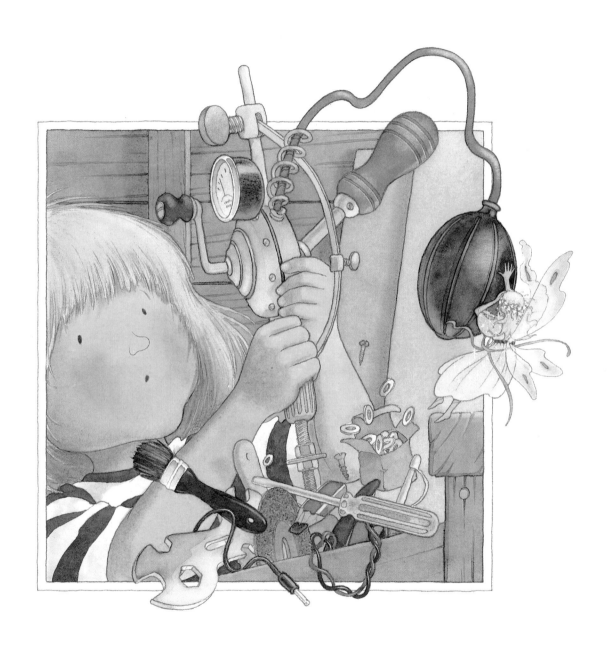

First published 1991
Second impression 1991
© Nick Butterworth 1991

A CIP catalogue record for this book
is available from the British Library

ISBN 0 00 191321 2

Printed and bound in Great Britain
by BPCC Paulton Books Limited

This book is set in Garamond